Survivors

By
Wolfgang Perner

Survivors

Contents

Dedication and acknowledgments

Chapter 1	On their way	1
Chapter 2	Red at morn, sailor be warned	9
Chapter 3	Making speed of the storm	18
Chapter 4	Survivor	22
Chapter 5	The arrangement	36
Chapter 6	Johnathan's camp	46
Chapter 7	Answers in the stars	51
Chapter 8	A ship	60
Chapter 9	Pirates!	64

ISBN-13: 978-0692080283

ISBN-10 :0692080287

Dedicated

to all the children and animals whose journeys

took an unexpected turn.

ii

Acknowledgment

I'm grateful to all my friends and family for encouraging me to publish this book, but especially to my wife Maryann.

On their way

The cries of gulls, the gentle caress of waves and the
rhythmic clunking of wooden boats gave way to the sound
of a distant foghorn. A mist hung in the brisk morning air.
There was no wind it seemed. Normally, stillness would be
good, because the wind just adds to the chill. But today was
not a day spent early in the fields, but a beginning of a
different sort.

Much planning had gone into this intercontinental voyage.
For years, hard work was endured for the eventual chance
to travel to a faraway place aglow with opportunity. It took
a long time to save for the fare and prepare all the things
that would be needed in the new country. Now all that work
has a whole family and all of their worldly goods stand in
the fog patiently waiting to load onto a ship.

The youngest in the family was Jonathan and the
anticipation of crossing the ocean made him too impatient
to stand around in the fog. He wanted to see the other ships.
The ship in front of him was good enough but he would be
on that ship for the next several weeks.

Some of the other ships on the dock looked far tidier and

their rigging looked like fine linen. Brass, shined to look as if it were gold, and hulls, shaped like fish no line could hold. The people who boarded those ships did not carry their own bags or wait with their cargo. The Shore men were loading the ship for others, who still slept soundly in goose-down at the local inn. Barrels of wine, ales, sides of pork, cabbages and bags of grains all going aboard, and luggage stored into appropriate cabins.

Jonathan was intrigued by all this activity and wanted to explore, but his father demanded everyone stay close by and out of the way of the frenzy. Ports were known to be places where one needs to have their wits about them.

Eventually the family's cargo was loaded into the small area allotted by the Captain for the passenger's belongings. The family had practiced this stacking on several occasions and some items had to be left behind to fit everything into a small space. There was no extra room in the tiny cabin that they had booked for the voyage. It was extra cramped because they had two chickens and two goats with them besides the family dog, "Scrappy".

Jonathan finally was free to explore, although now he was confined to a ship. Jonathan was hoping to make friends with the Captain who was not to be found. He asked the crew about his whereabouts and learned new words:

"starboard" and "port", "stern" and "aft". When he finally showed himself the Captain seemed a bit grumpy and looked as if he'd had a long night at the inn when he showed up to announce that the ship will sail on the tide.

"Well that answers it," Jonathan thought to himself. He had wondered how they were going to sail so far without a shred of wind. "Will we ever get out of this port?" he wondered all morning. Before he could imagine how a ship sails on the tide, they were on their way toward the moaning fog buoy.

Sails were lowered and made taut with a slight breeze and the ship swayed and creaked as speed increased and the gulls stopped landing on the rigging. Sails snapped in the wind and lines whipped. Waves shattered to mist and land became ever smaller on the horizon. Soon it all looked the same. In all directions, there was ocean.

In the cabin Jonathan's mother, Mary, had arranged the limited space well. The chicken cages fit under the bunk on one side while the goats would have to find space on the floor at night and be tied to a tether on deck during the day. The goats still provided milk and were too valuable to leave behind. Chickens were just part of the family.

Jonathan had to share the bunk with his father, also named Jonathan. Mary had a bunk to herself but somehow a

3

Jonathan or two would wake up there, Mary on the other side with Scrappy.

The little dog had his own little carrier box and was put in it every night, but he would usually be on the bed in the morning. His little body provided a bit of warmth on cold nights and was rarely noticed unless he snored or passed gas.

On the first night at sea, Scrappy was restless. He scratched and whined and did not like that there was no soil for him to do his business. He knew he could get in trouble if he went in the wrong place. In the morning he could not stand it any longer . He had to go now!

He ran back and forth on the deck and smelled something so horrific that he thought he could only improve it. It was a bucket that had obviously experienced this emergency before but offered little help to a small dog. "Good enough", thought Scrappy and he let go.

Worse things have happened on the decks of ships but they have never made a dog so happy. Jonathan was next and quickly cleaned Scrappy's mess too. Now the goats had to be tethered on deck. One by one Jonathan and his dad tied them to the hatch covers. The chickens were not allowed to run free either. They had to stay in their cages but were put out on deck to get fresh air and sun. It really helped

4

because chickens and goats do not smell so good.

The ship had an aroma also. It smelled of seaweed, spices, rope and wood. Sometimes the faint smell of burning tobacco rose from below the deck or the smell of an extinguished candle wick mixed with the scent of cedar timber.

This ship was no fancy passenger ship like the ones he had seen at the dock. This was a cargo ship, and an old one at that. It had traveled many miles and hauled many tons and its memoirs would fill books on their own. But this is not a book about a ship and I will not even tell of its name.

Passengers rarely travel on cargo ships. There is no staff to serve you. You eat what you brought if the rats don't beat you to it. The crew rotates the cooking among themselves in what is best described as "scrappin". Most sailors brought food or faced constant hunger. You had to constantly guard your food. Rations were small. Water was precious.

At the beginning of an ocean voyage it takes the body time to adjust to the motion of the ship and the rhythm of the waves. Some people don't eat. Some people become ill. Some hardly notice. It was late in the day when a chow bell rang and the crew assembled for a meal. Mary served sandwiches she had prepared the previous day. Food in

5

their bellies and a beautiful sky made the first day of the voyage very enjoyable and they were excited to be on their way.

As the evening progressed, everyone came up on deck to watch a beautiful sunset reflect on a calm ocean. The Captain spoke of favorable conditions and appointed the watch. Crew members played music, cards and dice or told stories of days gone by and places that Jonathan had never heard of.

Mary wanted Jonathan to come to the cabin and practice reading but Jonathan was more interested in the stories that the sailors told. It was probably best that he listen to Mary. He still had to bring in the animals so maybe he could just hear a little more?

By morning the ship was far from any land and in the far distance clouds looked like islands. The wind had picked up a little and the ship was moving well. An occasional slap and flutter of the sail broke the sound of the waves hitting the bow and bursting into streams of spray as the ship lifts and falls into the next.

The movement of the ship made balance difficult and added some comedy to using the bucket of necessity. Scrappy had no problem leaving an additional obstacle for Jonathan who was a doing a most curious dance with a very smelly bucket on a slippery deck.

This was very entertaining for the sailors and they laughed at Jonathan. They all remembered their first dance with the bucket and tried to offer advice. Nothing teaches like experience. "We'll make a sailor outa ye yet", they said. Somehow that got him a mop and pail and the dubious distinction as "swobby".

Of course, this job came with all sorts of nomenclature too exhaustive to delve into here and such will be avoided as this is not a story about being a sailor. Goats and chickens are incontinent, and that is truer at sea. Jonathan is finding that there are a lot of chores on ships. He has to take care of the animals and keep them clean too. At the end of the day he is as much crew as passenger.

Mary does not like it when he visits with the crew alone, but in the evening, everyone gathers on deck and socializes. Jonathan overhears tales of natives and pirates, tales never told on the continent, and wonders what awaits him as he brings his animals into the small ship's cabin for the night and goes to sleep.

Jonathan dreams of jungles and tigers, while Scrappy dreams of catching rats. Both slumber into paradise. Jonathan's Mom and Dad join them in sleep as the ship rolls into the night, gently creaking back and forth like an heirloom cradle. The faint smell of candle wick overpowers the smell of the chickens and goats and the sound of gentle snoring seems synchronized to the waves.

Red at morn, sailor be warned

Dawn was beautiful. Pink feathered clouds and tones of red and orange announced the rising sun. White-capped waves sprung wings and disappeared one after another for as far as the eye could see. The sails were tight and the ship slapped through them, a slight tilt to starboard.

It was cold and windy but everyone was on deck except the chickens. Jonathan kept them warm inside. Scrappy ran around the deck on a rat hunt until it drew him below deck. Hunting is serious business for a Jack Russell and Scrappy lived up to the legacy.

Rats know a lot about ships and have traveled the seven seas on them as long as ships have been around. They know all the good spots to hide. Jack Russells have a keen nose and can smell a rat from a great distance. Scrappy was so fixated on the rat that he forgot where he was. He was not supposed to go below deck, only crew was allowed.

Meanwhile Jonathan told a crew member about his adventurous dream, and in turn learned from him how to tie a knot three different ways. Jonathan had only tied up his goats and his shoelaces and did not know that there were so many knots. Sailors know a lot about knots. But this is not a book about knots.

Jonathan was not too worried about Scrappy because he was sure-footed as any dog and had a healthy respect for the edge of the deck. By the time he noticed that Scrappy had been gone awhile, the little dog had worked himself deep into the hold in the relentless pursuit of a rodent.

Jonathan searched and called and was feared some ill had happened to his pal. He asked the crew and Captain but no-one had seen Scrappy in hours.

As night fell and Jonathan was putting the other animals away for the night, he thought he heard Scrappy. Then he heard him again. Yes, that was him barking far away. Where is he? He could only be below deck somewhere. But what can Jonathan do? He is not allowed below. Jonathan knew he had to get Scrappy into the cabin before they went to bed.

The crew and Captain were singing loudly and a harmonica and accordion were playing. A bottle of rum was passed around and it helped lubricate a good time.

Jonathan went into the hold to look for Scrappy. As he got half way down the ladder he realized that he didn't have a candle with him or even a match. It was pitch black down there. But he could hear Scrappy. "Come here boy," he called quietly. Scrappy was not listening. Down a few more steps, and he called again. Come here boy," he called quietly. But he got no response but a slight whimper from Scrappy.

Feeling along in the dark and getting closer to Scrappy, Jonathan could smell a strong odor of pipe tobacco similar to what had been only a subtle aroma before. Then a noise, it was a door. Oh no, someone is coming. Jonathan's heart almost stopped, and then started beating very loudly. His heart was all he could hear. Then Scrappy jumped out and barked. "There you are ", Jonathan says. But Scrappy was on the attack.

The dark was broken by a light from an oil lamp carried by a man Jonathan had not seen on the ship before. "What are you doing here? Get this dog off me!"The man shouted. "You are not allowed down here, do you understand?" he yelled at Jonathan "You are to tell no one what you saw down here, do you understand?" Jonathan grabbed Scrappy and nodded that he understood. Scrappy kept growling.

All Jonathan had seen were crates and some bags of potatoes. He was glad that he had Scrappy back, and that the man did not tell anyone that he was caught down below.

11

He wondered about the man, but never mentioned him. He took Scrappy and put him in his carrier and went to sleep. Scrappy soon joined him. Another day came to an end with the ship never slowing.

At dawn the ship groaned and swayed and things slid back and forth a bit if they weren't tied down. Jonathan's Dad and Mom were using twine to secure things around the small cabin. The goats and chickens were not going onto the deck today. Scrappy was anxious about getting out.

When Jonathan opened the door it was ripped from his hand and slammed against the bulkhead. A wild gush of wind swirled around the tiny cabin and papers took flight. Just as suddenly the door slammed shut and the papers fluttered to rest.

"I think we are all going to stay in here ", Jonathan's Dad explained. "It's just too dangerous on deck today." The wind howled under the door in agreement. So, Jonathan snuggled up with Scrappy and picked up his shoe to practice his knots.

The ship swayed and crashed through waves, constantly tilting toward starboard. A bell rang as for chow, but more vigorously and with a different pattern. "Batten down, Batten down, Batten Down ,batten down," echoed down the chain of command as the crew scurried around on deck.

12

"Steady as she goes mates, we're in the winds," shouted the Captain, barely audible from the deck.

The monotony of the small cabin was interrupted by a very loud knock on the door. It was the Captain. When he opened the door, it was as if the wind slowed for just a moment and no papers took flight at all. He held the door steady and blocked the opening with his body as he spoke.

"Everybody getting along alright here? We're having a bit of luck with the wind and may save a few day's time at this rate. We apologize for the inconvenience ". Everyone nodded and smiled, and it wasn't until the door shut that all the questions came back to their minds.

Jonathan's Dad decided better get that stinky bucket. Yuck. After that business was all done a little crazy wind was welcomed. As the door once again slammed against the bulkhead upon opening, it sent papers adrift in the gust, blowing out Mary's candle.

It had become a bit stuffy, if you get my drift. Mary put her book away. The loose papers she saved were tied in a bundle with twine. After a shuffle of luggage, she tucked the bundle into her trunk and slid the chickens back under the bunk.

Jonathan had managed to get his shoelaces in a serious

13

tangle and Scrappy was trying to chew them apart on one shoe while Jonathan was using his teeth to pry the knot apart on the other. When Mary saw that, she was not happy. "What are you guys doing to those shoes? They are all you have Jonathan! You know how to tie shoes, what is this mess?" She pulled the left shoe from Scrappy's mouth just in time. Apparently, ship knots don't work well on shoelaces, or actually, they work too well.

Over the next few days, things remained the same, but the smell in the cabin got steadily worse. The ship groaned louder and the slapping waves became an ever faster beat. The crew could be heard working hard on deck scurrying about and repeating commands. It seemed they never slept. Day and night this went on and Jonathan lost count of the many days they were stuck in the cabin with goats and chickens.

Scrappy wanted out–he liked the wind. He sniffed under the door and whined, but Jonathan's Dad did not allow Jonathan to take him out on the deck. It was just too risky.

One morning Jonathan awoke and thought he was no longer on a ship. He thought he woke up in the old barn with the animals. There was no tilt to starboard, no wind whistling under the door, no waves slapping the ship, no crew running around on deck. What was going on?

Jonathan and Scrappy jumped up and opened the cabin door. Mary and Jonathan Sr. awoke too and they all saw a beautiful sunrise and an ocean that looked like the pond at home in the summer time.

"Oh thank goodness "Mary sighed. Jonathan took the goats out and let them loose on the deck, and released the chickens, too. The two hens immediately chased each other around the deck, running over a crew member who had passed out from exhaustion from the long run in the strong winds. He didn't notice.

The goats found some rope and chewed it but nobody seemed to mind now. It was so quiet and calm. Later in the day, the crew got up and about and a loud splash was heard. "Man over board!" was shouted and repeated in a cheerful tone followed by more splashes and laughter. "They're swimming, Mom they're swimming, I want to swim, Mom, I want to swim, please let me swim, Mom!" Jonathan shouted.

"Absolutely not, young man," was the reply. Then "Come on in boy" in the voice of Jonathan Sr. He was talking to Scrappy who had already jumped in with the crew. "Well, I guess it's alright, but stay with your father." She recanted. Seconds later Scrappy and Jonathan were swimming in the ocean with no land in sight.

The fresh air and bath cheered up spirits and improved the atmosphere considerably. Everyone but the Captain was very happy. He was grumbling about losing the days he had gained riding the strong wind.

The smell of pipe tobacco seemed to linger stronger than before. It sounded as if furniture was being arranged below, bumping and sliding. Jonathan wondered what was happening below deck, but did not ask. He did not want to admit he had been down there. The man with the pipe never came on deck and Jonathan was not sure who else knew of him.

By afternoon the wind had picked up and the ship was once again under full sail and making good speed. Now the ship was leaning to port and the bunks were rearranged with the pillows on the foot of the bunk to elevate the head while sleeping. The goats and chickens faced opposite, too. They were accustomed to the ship by now and slept well despite the leaning, rocking and constant slap of waves hitting the bow.

Morning came and went and the daily routine was almost second nature. The goats were tied on the deck and the chickens put out in their cages. Jonathan was getting good at tying knots and untying them, too. During the day he spent time on deck with the crew, learning about ships and some things about sailors, too." We'll make a sailor of you yet," they often promised, but Jonathan was not sure that he wanted to be a sailor. He knew he did not want to be a "Landlubber" whatever that was, because it didn't sound very good, but he really wanted to get off that ship.

Jonathan was bored. The ship seemed a lot larger the first day, but had shrunk over time. It was cramped and smelled like a barn with fish in it. He just imagined how beautiful it will be in the new country and how this is all worth the trip.

He knew he was lucky to have great parents and a dog, and goats that give milk and chickens that lay eggs, and all the best of their things are with them, too. He wondered how much longer they had to be on the ship. Were they still ahead of schedule?

Making speed of the storm

The wind must have heard Jonathan and howled under the door. The ship groaned in response and leaned hard to port. Sails snapped and lines creaked tight as the ship plunged in response and everyone braced to the stern. They were once again in the winds making speed. Overnight the wind increased. In the morning the wind pushed the door closed. Not only was it uphill to the door because the ship was leaning hard to port but the wind blew against the door from the north and held it shut. The breaking waves, with a steady pulse, mist the porthole window.

Soon the mist turned to rain and the sea became rough. Things tossed around in the cabin and ended up on the floor with the goats. There was no time to be bored. Everyone had to hold on. That night, nobody slept. Their thoughts were with the crew who was fighting to control the ship. Mary was worried. After all, the ship was quite old. Jonathan's Dad reassured her that the ship was a well-tested design and had made the trip many times.

The storm lasted for days and the cabin began to stink again. It was hard to sleep, and hard to go to the bucket. The weather was so bad that the crew could not be heard on the deck. Occasionally there was a crash, or a loud bump, but no voices. The wind's howl and rain's slap on the ship broke up the constant sound of breaking waves. Water came under the door and the goats were restless. Could this get any worse?

Jonathan was hoping to wake up to another calm day and take a swim perhaps. Scrappy was getting grumpy. Those chickens stunk, everybody stunk. The ship just kept going, it felt very fast. "How much longer until we get there?" Jonathan demanded. "We have been on this ship for weeks." The parents sighed and had no answer. "Soon I hope," Mary conceded, but she knew it would probably be a few more days.

They all knew that ship could not possibly go faster. In fact, their speed so far had been remarkable. Cargo ships are not normally known for speed. Not like those sleek ships at the dock. Dogs, goats, and chickens are not permitted on those fancy ships, and they could not leave them behind. Peasants do not travel on fancy ships, and all of their belongings would have to be left behind. The fare on those ships cost the wages of a year for a poor man and Jonathan Sr. was a wealthy man in all but wage. He preferred to have most of his things with him when he started anew in a far-away land of great opportunity.

The storm became so intense nobody noticed the stench of the animals and humans crowded in the tiny cabin.
 Sleep came for moments at a time and was interrupted by loud crashes of heavy things sliding back and forth below deck. Wind and rain whipped at the door and portholes and small waves of water were leaking in under the door.

Between waves the wind whistled. The chicken cages slid from side to side under the bunk, thudding to a stop in each direction, small waves of water splashing back and forth beneath them. The goats leaned against the wall to keep their bellies dry.

It became dark but it was useless to light a candle. Everyone felt ill. They had not eaten much because the storm made them queasy. There was no fresh air except the whistle under the door seam.

Scrappy was snoring with his back against Jonathan's leg. It sounded like he was dreaming, a light growl followed by a whimper and blinking and squinting his eyes. His front paws moved alternately as if to mimic running or digging. Jonathan wanted sleep, too, but the ship tossed too much.

Out of nowhere Jonathan was thrown forward and hit by a very warm wave of water. Then came another surge of water. Everything was upside down, rolling like a barrel, water washing back and forth. Around they went again and this time with a huge bang and a lot more water. Water was everywhere. Which way is up? Something hit Jonathan in the head. "Ouch!" he yelled as water filled his mouth. He choked.

He coughed, swallowed more water. Another knock to the head, more water, and he could not breathe.

A bright light appeared.

The ship sailed at full speed into an island. It hit the rocks so hard that it flipped the ship over a reef, smashing it into little pieces. All was lost it seemed, scattered on the beach of an island that was not known to be there. Debris washed up on the shore and spread out along the beach and on the rocks.

Sharks gathered and scavenged the wreckage and seabirds inspected the flotsam. Hours went by as the wreck continued to break apart. More and more washed up. Seagulls dragged their finds out of the surf but quickly lost interest. The sharks had better luck.

Survivor

Wet sand has a smell that is hard to mistake. Pleasant, not too strong, but unique. Salt water has a bad taste. It was the alternating smell of sand and the nasty taste of seawater that brought Jonathan back to consciousness. What seemed blissful for a moment was soon a mouthful of sand and saltwater. A wave of surf reminded him of his sudden awakening during the crash. Spitting and coughing, he crawled to his feet and came to rest on a white beach.

The sun was just coming up. Warm rays were shining on Jonathan's wet skin and it felt good. "Where am I?" he wondered. "MOM!, DAD! Scrappy!" he yelled, realizing he was shipwrecked, "Where are you!?" he cried. Jonathan stood and surveyed the beach with tearful eyes. Where was everybody? Were they alive? Did anyone else survive?

Debris was scattered for a long distance. Wood was bobbing in the surf along with what appeared to be crates. A few things were lying on the beach that Jonathan recognized, among them the book and papers that Mary had tied into a bundle with twine on the ship. He picked it up and cried.

"MOM! DAD! Scrappy!" he cried. There was no answer.

As the sun rose, Jonathan stopped crying and shivering. He walked up and down the beach in the warmth, calling for his family. Then he smelled something familiar. Smoke. That means maybe someone else survived. Hope came over Jonathan.

The smoke was blowing around a point to the north, beyond rocks that blocked his view. He ran to see who was there, relieved that he was not alone.

When he neared the point, he heard Scrappy. "Scrappy!" he called, half crying and half laughing. Relief. Scrappy bounced over the rocks and Jonathan fell to his knees. "Oh, Scrappy, you're safe." He whimpered and was overcome with tears. "Mom!" he called once again, "Dad? Where are you?" There was licking and tail wagging, and Scrappy was happy to be found.

Boy and dog ran to the top of the rocks to see the other side hoping that his parents were there at the fire.

When they came to the top of the ridge, the smell of smoke was strong. It made the eyes burn and and the lungs cough. Jonathan had smoke in his eyes and could not see well as he got his first glimpse of the beach beyond the rocks.

"Well whom 'av we here?" the raspy voice of the Captain

bellowed from the smoke.

"Jonathan the sailor is it? And his little rat chaser."

"Have you seen my Mom and Dad?" Jonathan demanded of the Captain. "Where are they, where are we, what happened?"

The Captain had no answers. "There's only one other survivor that I know of," the Captain said, pointing to the man whom Jonathan had seen below deck way out in the waves, trying to drag a crate back with him. "Go on sailor, give him a hand," the Captain commanded, pointing to the man.

Scrappy barked disapproval at the Captain and ran to the surf to bark at the man wrestling with the crate, who was trying to swim back with it. "Oh hush Scrappy," Jonathan commanded his pal as he marched into the waves. Scrappy barked the whole time but would not get in the water.

Jonathan was a good swimmer and easily reached the man with the crate, who looked exhausted and glad to get help. "Help me get this ashore," the man barked, as Scrappy continued his protest. When they reached shore, Scrappy continued to bark his dislike of the man and the Captain.

It sank in–Jonathan lost his parents in the shipwreck He felt an intense sadness. They had worked and planned for a future in a great new country, but now that all changed. The two pals walked the beach together, searching for anything, but most of all their Mom and Dad. By night fall they were losing hope.

The Captain and the man with the crate from below the ship had found their rum and busied themselves celebrating their survival. They became louder as the night progressed and more boisterous as well. They spoke of things that Jonathan had never heard, and Scrappy growled softly under his breath every time they raised their voices.

Jonathan and Scrappy had laid their heads down and were trying to sleep. But the men were getting louder. They started to argue about who owned the wreckage and how the salvage was to be divided. Back and forth went claims and accusations, insinuations and confessions.

Jonathan wondered if they were going to take his things, too. Some of the salvage on the beach belonged to his family. All this made it difficult to sleep. Slumbering, Jonathan heard his name. He sat up. Scrappy growled.

"What of the lad?" was the current topic. "Crew and passengers belong to the ship!" the Captain asserted, while the man from below deck, whom the Captain refers to as "Coronel," argued that Jonathan and any other survivors were on their own, and should have to fend for themselves.

"We both need the help of the lad, and anyone else that comes along to get all this salvage up on the beach." the Captain argued. "We can't let the surf take it." Coronel agreed. Both men wanted their property; however, Jonathan yearned for his Mom and Dad.

Scrappy was dreaming about chasing rats below deck and smelling a cat. His legs were kicking spasmodically, and he huffed between snores and whimpered on the exhale. Jonathan lay awake, and wondered what was happening in Scrappy's dream until he, too, finally found sleep in the warm sand.

The rum had taken its toll on the men and they passed out. Their snores kept rhythm with the waves and each other. The smell of fire gave way to fresh morning breeze and the call of sandpipers. Gulls joined. Soon the sun was beating on eyelids, and the smell of sand and seaweed announced the new day to the other senses. Stirring, stretching, yawning and wiping sand from the face, everybody came to their feet and looked out over the vast ocean. Greeting with a silent wave they drew closer to where the fire was.

Debris littered the beach. Along the rocks, wooden images were interspersed between seaweed and mussels. The waves broke over them and the wood shifted and rolled between rocks. Some of it was lumber from the broken ship and some was cargo. Few useful items lay in shallow surf, bobbing and rolling with each wave. There was no sign of other survivors.

"See anyone else?" the Captain inquired in a loud voice above the crashing waves. Shaking dropped heads were the only answer besides the loud shriek of an albatross and an especially loud crash in the surf. "Well let's get as much of this wreck on the beach as possible," the Captain ordered.

"What of my cargo? You are obligated to save my cargo first, Captain; your ship can not be saved," Coronel roared, in combative protest, charging toward the Captain.

Jonathan tried to stay out of the argument, but Scrappy would have none of it. He barked and snapped at the heels of the aggressors until calm was restored. "Ye had best control yer little rat catcher, if ye knows what's good," the Captain sneered. "First the surf checked for salvage and survivors, then we'll tend t' yer precious cargo Mate." and so it was.

The immediate task did not need discussing, or anyone to take charge. All were hoping to see any survivor, but Jonathan especially wanted his family. Walking along the edge of the waves that licked the beach, Jonathan and Scrappy picked up anything that looked usable and tossed or placed, sometimes dragged what they found out of the reach of the ocean. The salvage needed to be saved, starting with things still being washed around in the surf.

The Captain was scanning for his crew and anything he could salvage as well. Coronel just waded out into the surf and swam out to where he believed the crates of cargo were lodged. Soon, he shouted inaudibly and waved as he sank below the waves and reappeared between them.

He had found something and was not letting it go. "Aye, he's barnacled to his precious cargo lad, 'tis best we help him heave to if it's so important," the Captain said, walking into the surf as if marching at the head of a parade. Jonathan followed.

Long swells turned to crashing whitecaps as they met the reef. Foam and turbulence washed chaotically over mussel-covered rocks, followed by brief periods of relative calm, and then repeated. The rhythm changes, but is endless. Several wave cycles later, they arrived at Coronel's first of many crates that had some mysterious importance. One by one the crates were located and dragged over the rocks through the surf until they could be no longer be moved, due to the soft, dry sand.

This brought joy to Coronel and relief to the Captain, but did little for Jonathan, who wanted to look around the other side of the island for his Mom and Dad. He was glad to find a few of his family's possessions, but wanted to make sure he had looked everywhere for his family.

"Now for me ship, mates, 'elp me pull'er ashore," the Captain demanded and marched back into the waves. Shaking their heads, Jonathan and the Coronel followed reluctantly into the turbulent tide to retrieve the pieces of the old ship, sails, rigging, timber and wares.

Several times sharks were spotted, but the lowered tide prevented them from coming close. Scrappy, safe on shore, kept an eye out and would bark and pace if he saw one. After the shipwreck, he never got into the water again.

Days went by and nights fell and went until no more debris was visible anywhere near the water. Two very distinct piles were formed on the high ground. One belonged to the Captain and was mainly made up of wreckage. Sails hung like tents over the top timbers tied together with rigging. Wood and timbers were stacked to break the wind. Down the beach, a large pile of crates was dragged and carried, one at a time, to higher ground.

Jonathan had found some of his family's things, too, and they were not a large pile at all. A small crate that Coronel mistook for his own had some pots and pans and basic kitchen utensils that Jonathan claimed. A cart that they had used to bring their belongings to the dock had washed up.

Some clothing and wood tools, a shovel, hoe, and a broken chicken cage is all he had, besides Scrappy, of course.

With all the salvage work apparently done, everyone wanted a day of rest and contemplation. They had developed different ideas about what to do next and weren't getting along well. It was obvious that everyone wanted time alone. They had worked hard and needed a break.

The Captain was building a shelter for himself that he referred to as "me ship". If anyone came near it, he became hostile. Sometimes he would struggle with a heavy piece and curse at the timbers. He liked to give orders, but did not know how to ask for help.

Coronel, a secretive man, was concerned with getting his cargo to a more private location. He could not move the crates alone and he did not seem to want to open them in front of anyone, either. He slept near the crates and seems to distrust the Captain.

Jonathan wanted to look on the other side of the island for his Mom and Dad. None of the survivors had been away from the beaches and rocks near the wreck. There was too much work to do, but now was Jonathan and Scrappy's chance to explore.

While the two men were busy with their projects, Scrappy

and Jonathan went off to look for Mary and Jonathan Sr. and to find out what this island was really like. Jonathan picked up a few of the potatoes that had washed up, put them in his pocket and off they went along the beach away from the wreckage, toward the south.

Tropical islands are dream destinations, but nobody wants to shipwreck on one. For now, Jonathan's dreams are nightmares. He felt lost, and he was lost at sea, for all anyone knew. Exploring a new place can settle the mind and few things are as distracting as natural beauty. This island was packed with it.

As the two pals rounded the southern tip of the small island, a beautiful cove appeared. On one side a white beach, sheltered by rocks. From a cliff, crystal clear water falls into a pool and disappears below the sand. Sea shells lay on the warm sand as palm trees wave sublimely in the breeze. Seabirds glide above the swell, occasionally dip to catch a fish.

Above the cliff, tropical plants droop with fruit that Jonathan did not recognize. Some birds appeared and made a commotion over them and their color drew curiosity. The thought of fresh food made Jonathan hungry. He had only eaten food that washed up from the wreck until now.

The cliff is slippery, but roots droop from the top to the beach. They made it easy for Jonathan to climb to the top. It was tougher for Scrappy. As they climbed, swallows that had nests in the cliff became upset and flew at them chirping and diving in defense of their abodes.

When they reached the lush jungle above the cove, he was amazed at all the different fruits in such a small area and the abundance of each. He did not know which fruit to eat so he started with the ones that the birds were eating. They were delicious! Scrappy liked them too, but he only ate one.

Jonathan ate a few and put some in his pocket to share when he returned to the wreckage. They had to crawl and climb to get through the dense, but small, jungle. The island did not have many bugs or pests. The only animals seen so far have been birds, lots of birds.

Many plants that grew on the island were unfamiliar. There did not appear to be any reptiles, but Jonathan kept an eye out for snakes. He had never seen a snake but had heard that they exist on tropical islands. He was a little scared. "Scrappy stay close," he said, slapping his thigh with his hand. Scrappy was already there and gave him a lick on the hand.

Soon, light shone in beneath the foliage and the other side

of the island came into view. As they approached the opening in the foliage, the ocean spread out to fill the horizon and they came to another cliff. This time, the climb was rocky and jagged and led to a boulder shore without sand.

Scanning the rocks below revealed a familiar sight. It was a crate that Jonathan Sr. had brought, but it was busted open and floating in a pool between some rocks. The lid was floating with the inside up and the box was on its side laying open, still attached by the hinges. It looked empty.

"Mom! Dad!" called Jonathan in desperate hope, while looking at the open crate floating in the Ocean. "Bahaharrrk," "mahhahaha," sounded from the crate. The goats and chickens had survived and were still floating in the spilled crate, lodged between rocks days after the storm. "Hey!" Jonathan screamed in excitement as he and Scrappy ran toward the water. "You guys are alive," he said in amazement as he waded into the pool.

A few feet from the rock, Jonathan realized he was in trouble. The current carried him into a big whirlpool that trapped the crate and Jonathan in a big spin. Round and round they went in a circle with every wave giving a little push. Jonathan could not reach the crate, much less swim back to the rocks. He quickly tired. The goats cheered him on, Scrappy barked from the shore.

Jonathan hoped no sharks would come. Things looked pretty dismal. "Help!" Jonathan screamed. The goats stared and the chickens paced. After a long swim, Jonathan finally got hold of the lid and pulled himself to it. When he tried to climb up, the crate nearly flipped and he quickly stopped. He kicked his feet to push the floating crate toward the edge of the pool. With much effort and Scrappy's encouragement, he made it to the rocks and got the animals safely to shore.

Jonathan felt accomplished and heroic with the rescue and the day was ending. He had to figure out how to get his animals back to the wreckage. It would not be easy with those cliffs, but they could not stray too far on the small island, so Jonathan decided to leave them and return for them one at a time. He headed back with new enthusiasm and joy at finding the animals and food.

He barely had time to move them to the top of the cliffs and into the cover of the trees before dark. By the time he brought them water and food only the stars lit his way.

Jonathan hurried back to share the food and good news about the animals. It was dark already and he had lost track of time, but enjoyed the day. He wondered what the two men had done while he was gone, and could not wait to tell them what he had found. He was sure the men would be happy, too.

The arrangement

Jonathan and Scrappy returned and heard the men argue so they decided to stay back and find a place to sleep away from the fire. The Captain and Coronel fought over who would be in charge, and who would be able to use Jonathan's help. They both knew he could be helpful, but neither wanted to treat him as a partner. They planned to use him, and the men were not used to asking nicely.

Coronel was yelling at the Captain that he was in charge and it was his expedition and that the Captain was not in charge on land. The Captain argued that while shipwrecked, the Captain does keep his charge and Coronel and Jonathan were passengers on his ship. Therefore, they shall take orders from him.

The Captain also attempted to take possession of all the salvage and food from the ship. Coronel suggested that the Ship's debris and anything belonging to the ship be the Captain's, but food be split up equally between the Captain and Coronel. They would then use the food to pay Jonathan for work. The Captain disagreed and said Jonathan can work for dirt since he's just a farmer's lad.

Jonathan tried to imagine what he might do with a bunch of dirt at the end of a busy day and where he would put it. He thought it would be nice to have a little place to live with his animals and his parents on top of the hill by the little jungle with the fruit trees.

As the men became more boisterous, all kinds of nasty ideas passed their lips about how they would treat Jonathan and how annoyed they were with Scrappy. They even said he might taste good. Jonathan heard every word because the men were drunk and loud and paid no attention to Jonathan's whereabouts.

Late in the evening the men decided to split the island in half except to give Jonathan a place in the middle so that he could be their servant. The nice beaches at each end of the island would be theirs and the part in the middle with steep cliffs would be Jonathan's. He would work for one in the morning and the other in the afternoon and each would pay him dirt. They laughed and shook hands, it was a deal.

As the men quieted, Jonathan contemplated what he heard and how it would affect his future. He trusted that everything would be alright and that the men would not hurt him and Scrappy. Already things were getting better, he had found food and saved his animals. Now he just had to find his parents. His Dad would be a big help right now and he really missed his Mom. He decided not to tell the men about finding his animals because they might eat them.

The next morning came with a seagull's cry answered by Scrappy's shrieking bark. After calming the little protector, Jonathan laid back and collected his thoughts before jumping up with the realization that he needed to find his parents. Quickly he jumped up and put on his boots and cleaned up his makeshift bed. He and Scrappy set out again to comb the beach for any sign of the parents.

Having no luck finding the parents, they went back to the place where the chickens and goats were to find them eagerly waiting. He knew the Captain was also eagerly waiting, so he provided them with water and promised to come back soon.

As he approached the fire after an unsuccessful search, the Captain barked orders at Jonathan to carry some salvaged planks up to the Captain's campsite. "Captain's quarters will be up on me bluff 'bove the waves on the north point," he explained in a gruff tone, "and Coronel's will be on the southern bluff."

"Ye shall make yer camp up on the cliff and report for duty every morn to meself and 'ery afternoon to Coronel." "And what shall I be paid?" asked Jonathan, sarcastically. "Dirt!"

yelled the Captain, "get moving!" Jonathan gladly obliged because things were actually working out , except that he was missing his parents.

He worked hard for the Captain, moving many things to the northern bluff and then made lunch for the Captain from the salted pork that the Captain found on the beach. The Captain ate most of it and tossed the bone to Jonathan and Scrappy. Jonathan loaded his cart with dirt as payment as the Captain chuckled, and tried to take it to the place where he had left his goats and chickens. But his trail was going to need some work.

Those men had just agreed to pay Jonathan with the most valuable thing on an island, topsoil. Jonathan let Scrappy have the bone although it was a little salty for a dog and he ate the fruit from the jungle. Lunch was short for him and Coronel was waiting.

Coronel had many crates that he wanted moved to the southern bluff. Jonathan brought his cart and moved crates almost until sunset. The crates were not heavy with the cart and as he cleared the trail of rocks and branches it became easier with every trip. When Coronel was tired, Jonathan collected his "dirt" and went back to his site to arrange himself a camp.

His soil had to remain as a pile on the high beach until the trail is improved. He was so tired that some soft ground was good enough and his trail was going to have to wait for now.

As Jonathan approached the Captain's makeshift "ship" the sun was just cresting the cliff. The old sailor was up and hungry and had started to chew on salted pork saved from the waves a few days prior. Aside from that, a few potatoes was all he had for food.

Jonathan offered him some jungle fruit, but he was very suspicious. "Try to poison me for me grub, are ye?" the Captain asked in a gruff but empathetic voice. "Oh no", Jonathan answered, "I was sharing food." "Then let's see ye 'ave a go mate", the Captain snarled.

Jonathan ate the fruit in two bites and wiped his face with his forearm after putting the seed in his pocket. "Hey! What was that?" asked the Captain with regret. "Don't know, but it was delicious," was Jonathan's reply.

"Well now go 'n fetch me some" was the first order of the day, and Jonathan and Scrappy went off to the little jungle to find fruit for the Captain. It was just a short way to the path that went up to the top off the waterfall and into the dense brush that gave way to the jungle facing east.

40

Jonathan found the fruit quickly and noticed that were some berries as well, but no birds were eating the berries. He decided to leave those berries alone for now. A little bit into the jungle, they noticed vines and trees with thorns, and tall grasses that could be used to build things.

Jonathan realized he was spending a lot of time and that he should return. When he got back to the "ship" with the fruit. The Captain was happy to see him and gladly ate the fruit. "Bring me some fruit ev'ry morn lad, won't ye", the Captain said, in the nicest tone he has used in days.

Jonathan and Scrappy spent the remainder of the morning moving salvage up to the "ship" for the Captain. The more of his things he gathered around him the happier he seemed to get. The old barnacle appears to have a soft side, so to speak.

The morning went quite well and Jonathan collected his cart-load of "dirt" and went where he planned to put the path to his camp, dropping it off on his way to work for Coronel, who was walking toward the crates on the beach.

"Just where are you off to sailor?" Coronel squawked at Jonathan, who was pulling the cart toward the recently plotted path to the little jungle. "Be right back Coronel,"

Jonathan answered, attempting to pick up his pace.

"Don't dally lad," Coronel ordered and continued to make his way on the moist sand toward the pile of salvaged crates to be moved to his portion of the island, as far from the Captain as land would allow.

When Jonathan returned to the beach with Scrappy, Coronel ordered the crates moved to his place on the southern bluff.

It sounded complicated to Jonathan, but he followed the instructions as well as he could. When all the crates were on the southern bluff, Coronel made Jonathan switch around the way the crates were stacked and placed. Jonathan wondered if he had stacked them wrong or if Coronel had simply changed his mind. It was not discussed and really did not matter to Jonathan at the end of the day.

Coronel did not open any crates in front of Jonathan, but it was obvious that he really wanted to see if everything had survived in them. He sent Jonathan and Scrappy home to their camp early, so he could have privacy. Jonathan collected his cart full of topsoil and went to feed his goats and chickens for the evening.

He carried water back to his camp and shared it with the goats and chickens. Scrappy needed a drink, too. Jonathan did not have enough bowls to let everyone have one, and he was using his pot to cook a couple of eggs that the chickens had laid. He shared with Scrappy, who was also very hungry.

In the distance, banging could be heard from the Captain busting wood for his fire and occasionally a nail squeaked from the opposite direction as Coronel pulled open his crates. With a some work on the trail, the cart was brought to the top of the cliff with a full load of soil. Jonathan piled up his topsoil and planted little pieces of potato and the seeds he saved. He brought water for his new little garden before he fluffed his bed and went to sleep.

Every morning, Jonathan reported to work and improved the living situation of both the Captain and Coronel. He carried most of the debris and salvage they claimed and arranged it in a sturdy shelter that kept them out of the weather. After hours, he built his own shelter, and attachment for his animals that reminded him of the house and barn at his home. Of course, it was much smaller and more primitive.

The Captain's "ship" looked very comfortable, although it could hold out no water except rain. It looked like a ship from a distance, perched on a clump of rocks. The sails formed a tent with a hammock below and walls surrounding it serving as a wind break. Stacked rocks made a nice place for the fire on chilly nights and a cooking spot, although the Captain never cooked. A driftwood log was placed by the fire like a bench that was sometimes sat on, sometimes used as a backrest and sometimes used as a table.

The Captain was a grumpy man, but seemed happier to see Jonathan. Scrappy didn't like the Captain and barked at him often. Sometimes the Captain would bark back, as a little dog."Arf arf," or as a big dog "Wroof wroof wroof!" Scrappy hated it and got angrier.

Coronel's place at the opposite side of the island was getting more comfortable as well. Most of his shelter was built of crates that were reassembled as a small cabin. And it was furnished with the smaller ones.

Coronel had a fire spot too, but his was better protected from the wind than the Captain's by stacking the rocks tall in a cone with an opening like an oven. Around the perimeter of his camp, he had laid out some books to dry. They were open with rocks weighing down the covers from the inside and the pages blowing back and forth in the wind like busy reference manuals in a library for spirits.

He is a busy man, that is easily startled, but he is also fond

44

of Jonathan's daily shift and the fruit Jonathan brings. Much has been accomplished, yet the future is very uncertain. He is a lot more at ease with the cargo being away from the Captain and safely stored for now but he still guards the secret of the contents. He has a comfortable bed, which Jonathan made from dried grasses and a piece of torn sail that the Captain did not mind being taken.

Good sleep makes for better days and everyone seemed to be getting along a little better. But Jonathan still did not mention his goats or chickens for fear that the Captain and Coronel would eat them.

Jonathan's camp

Jonathan and Scrappy were busy with the work for the Captain and Coronel but they were still able to work on their own camp, too. It became better with every day. The goats became more comfortable and gave more milk. The chickens provided eggs. Jonathan needed more sail to use for blankets for his bed. He could use one of those glass containers for his milk, too.

He was afraid to offer a trade for milk and eggs, because he didn't trust the men. He had to find another way to trade for those things. He picked a large amount of fruit for Coronel and offered to trade for a fancy glass flask but was refused. He tried to offer the fruit to the Captain for a piece of torn sail, but the Captain refused as well. Instead, he made a roof and walls of palm leaves.

He soon built a bigger place with the palm leaves he collected and made a little pen for the goats and chickens to run around in during the day. He made a fireplace like the one he built for Coronel and carried driftwood from the beach to burn. At night, he snuggled with Scrappy and dreams of his parents and the beautiful place they had sought in their travels.

Jonathan took good care of all his animals. He gave them shelter and plenty of food. He has plenty of fruit for his chickens, and he stripped branches to be used for building and fed the tender parts to the goats. Sometimes, he walked with them and let them graze. The chickens came on the walks, too, and pecked at the trail, eating scarce bugs and seeds. Scrappy got milk and eggs and he ate fruit, too.

The pile of grasses that Jonathan used to build his bed grew loftier and more comfortable, especially after a hard day's work He looked forward to its comfort. Sometimes it was hard to get up in time to work and still feed all the animals in the morning, but Jonathan could go until everyone at his camp was fed.

The men had not been sharing their food with Scrappy and Jonathan and Jonathan had not told them about the chickens and goats. A small garden emerged at Jonathan's camp, because every day he brought home two carts loaded with of soil, potato scraps and all the seeds he could salvage. The soil he chose was fertile and came from centuries of sea bird droppings. Seedlings emerged quickly and the potatoes spread out a little bit more with each new day.

In the morning, dewy mists arose and he rarely had to carry water to his garden. He mixed chicken droppings with goat manure to make compost to fertilize his garden even more. Before he added the compost, earthworms found the garden and enriched it, too.

Even though the men hoarded their food, they nearly ran out. Jonathan's food supply looked better all the time. The Captain and Coronel were eating the berries Jonathan brought with increased enthusiasm as their food supply from the ship dwindled, but did not offer Jonathan any of the rations.

Jonathan was happy to be eating and to have his friends. He was happy to be useful and hardly noticed that the men are not reciprocating. He worried more about guarding his animal friends from them.

As the weeks added up on the island without rescue, the food supply salvaged from the ship ran out. The salted ham had run out long ago, as did the smoked fish, but now the potatoes were gone, too.

The Captain threatened to eat Scrappy, but it was obvious that he couldn't catch him. Scrappy ran circles around the Captain until the Captain fell in the sand, cursing. Jonathan brought berries and fruit and kept the men happy for the time being. The Captain told Jonathan to take some reeds and weave a basket to catch fish.

Jonathan had never trapped fish, and the basket did not work. He tried to change the trap, but had little luck, until Coronel saw what he was trying to do. In a few hours, Jonathan was catching fish in his new trap, but the Captain claimed the trap for himself, and Coronel argued it was his plan that made it work. Neither of the men acknowledges that Jonathan is the one who actually caught the fish.

Finally, the men decided that they would share the fish, and after some fast talking on Jonathan's part they agreed to let Jonathan have every fifth fish that he caught. With the shelters built and supplies stored, the focus quickly shifted to food. There was little to do on the island, but to hope for rescue and to eat. This was especially true for the Captain and Coronel who had a servant and nothing to do. Jonathan had to work to feed everyone.

The schedule changed from a split shift to serving meals twice daily for the men at their compounds. Every day that Jonathan fed the men he would take his payment of one cart load of soil to his camp and plant any seeds he found or saved in the soil.

He would add the fish waste to the compost or feed it to

the chickens and very little ever went to waste. The men were happy with the meals and never thought about how Jonathan was getting along or what he was doing with all that soil.

Jonathan on the other hand was a farmer from the start and had been growing a large garden in all the soil he worked. He had no complaints and hardly noticed that the men had run out of the food from the ship.

He just kept working on his garden and improving his soil. He cherished every seed and had faith that they would grow. He nurtured every plant and every start and they produced for him. Soil came faster than the roots could grow and it got better all the time.

The men had become so spoiled by Jonathan's cooking that they did not notice that he had started to include milk and eggs in some of the dishes. Fish had become a regular item on the menu. Although the men were healthy, they complained about the foods they no longer had, as if they were better. Jonathan however, had nothing but gratitude.

Answers in the stars

Several months had passed since the shipwreck landed the survivors on the island. Jonathan had been paid in soil for his hard work. He built shelters for everyone, and fed them, too, his only pay soil and scant appreciation. But he used the soil to create a beautiful garden.

Three people and a few animals can only consume so much food, and to plant more is just silly. Why would anyone want to work more than is necessary? Jonathan had enough soil and compost, he didn't need more.

But the men still needed to eat. Jonathan didn't know what to do. He did not want to keep moving soil to his camp. His garden was large enough and the men did not have much that Jonathan wanted. He didn't like rum or tobacco and they were nearly gone anyway. Everything the men had, he helped them build.

He did want a few more glass flasks, but they were no longer important–he has been happy without them for months. He found a better material than torn sails for his shelter, so he didn't need them anymore. Basically, the men ran out of anything to pay Jonathan. Why should Jonathan keep feeding the Captain and Coronel? What can he ask in return for his work now? What will the men offer when they get hungry?

The stars above slowly moved across the sky as Jonathan contemplated his future and worried about how the men will react. He wished for sleep but stared instead into the vast field of stars, reaching for an answer now from light years away.

In the morning, Jonathan rose early and fed the animals. He milked his goat and found a single egg. He suspected that his hen was hiding eggs somewhere, but another matter worried him. Hurrying along, he and Scrappy ate the egg, drank the milk, and picked greens and fruit to make a salad. He shared it with the Captain and Coronel. This day the Captain was going to get an early visit.

The Captain was grumpy and elusive. Jonathan thought he was going to be figuring out their location. The Captain mumbled about equator and various stars, but he would not answer questions. He kept saying he needed to know the date. "How many days out?" he kept repeating. Jonathan had lost count. Much too long, he thought.

Later in the day, Jonathan asked Coronel to remember how long they had been on the journey, but he could not remember for sure, either. He said they should see the season change soon.

"What does that mean?" Jonathan thought almost out loud. Jonathan hoped that did not mean snow. Back home on the farm it snowed sometimes in the winter, even late fall occasionally. What he did not know is that hurricane season could start any day.

The Captain has an epiphany and thought he may know where they were . He saw the moon midday and calculated from the full moon from the passage. Every full moon takes 28 days and every quarter, seven. A few rounds of counting on fingers and toes, and the Captain thinks he knows. But the Captain does not tell, and keeps his calculation to himself. He draws figures in the sand, places a stick to cast a shadow and learns where they are.

He had a plan, but he told Jonathan not to bother him. A few days passed and neither the Captain nor Coronel noticed that Jonathan did not bring very much food. It had been very hot, and nobody was that hungry.

The Captain, however, was secretly very busy. He tied the larger timbers together into a small raft. He used smaller wood to build a sail with a solid piece of canvas. He was busy building a raft for himself only and did not want anyone to see. He was obsessed with it.

Jonathan didn't mind, he hadn't noticed. He was at his own shelter worrying about the seasons changing.

"How can we survive a winter here?" he thought. Scrappy sensed Jonathan's worry, and dug a giant hole. It probably made great dog sense, but to Jonathan it was just a big dusty mess.

Jonathan had tried to count the days that had passed since that day on the dock in the morning fog. He counted over and over, but the first few weeks after the shipwreck, he was in mourning. When someone is very upset, time seems to stand still.

He came up with an answer, thinking he knew the exact number of days.

"C'mon Scrappy, let's go see the Captain!" he yelled in joy, as he led the way down to the beach. He was so thrilled he ran almost all the way to the far side of the point where the Captain had his "ship".

But the "ship" had sailed. The Captain was nowhere to be seen and much of his shelter was gone as well. "CAPTAIN!" Jonathan yelled at the top of his lungs several times before he realized the Captain was gone.

54

All the large timbers that had been salvaged from the wreck were gone, the sail canvas was gone, the rope was gone, and of course the Captain's favorite things were gone, too. The Captain left and took what he wanted with him. Jonathan, used to the grumpy old guy, now felt sad that he left.

Jonathan went to Coronel's camp and told him the Captain had left. He didn't know for sure, but he knew what he didn't see–the Captain and all his things were gone. Coronel was surprised at the news and went to see for himself. It was obvious that the Captain sailed off on a small raft, but to where? Was it related to the position of the island?

Did he realize he was close to land? They agreed the Captain must have known where he was when he left. They were disappointed he abandoned them.

Coronel told Jonathan about how he met the Captain. He told of paying him money to bring him to the land of his birth. That the Captain said he recognized the story of Coronel's people and would take him to their home.

He did not have enough money on his own, so he made a deal with a rich man to finance the voyage in return for samples of medicinal plants. That is why he has all those crates and glass containers.

They were supposed to protect the samples for the return trip. Coronel did not want anyone else on the ship, but the Captain took Jonathan's family along for the extra money. That is why they were so cramped. The voyage was secret, because the financier did not want to draw attention or competition. Although the Captain got all the money, the responsibility was all Coronel's.

He owed the financier a large sum of money or an equitable number of samples, and now he was unsure he could deliver on his promises. All he really wanted was to see if he still had family in the place of his birth. He was taken away as a small child and raised by wealthy Europeans, but he always missed the place from where he came.

He had fond memories of his grandmother, and how she could cure any illness with plants. He remembered eating from the trees and said Jonathan had brought back the memories when he gave him the food on the island.

Jonathan told Coronel about the goats and chickens, and explained he thought the Captain would eat his friends. They both laugh out loud and embraced. Coronel said, "Don't worry, they are safe." Scrappy licked his hand.

Jonathan was eager to share the plants he had been serving.

He gathered a good branch from one the plants and prepared it for drying by putting it his mother's book. He brought some fruit as well and laid slices on a rock to dry. But, the most important part was to save the seeds.

When he presented the plant, seeds and fruit to Coronel he was met with a large smile. It was the first sample. Although it technically was not a known medicine, it helped them survive a shipwreck.

Coronel carefully recorded the details on a small piece of paper; paper had become very precious since they had very little. Then he sealed it in a flask by melting bee's wax he had brought and dipped the mouth and cork in it.

Coronel glowed with joy for the first time since Jonathan had met him. "Can we collect more?" he asked. Jonathan was happy to contribute. It seemed like they had a purpose for being there.

Over the next couple of weeks, the two survivors spent much time together, gathering, drying, labeling and naming plants. They even found plants that Jonathan had not noticed before. Jonathan no longer feared for his companions. He was happy to show his camp to Coronel, who was very impressed.

Fear and distrust was replaced with trust and cooperation

and now the goats could roam free during the day. It didn't take long before the goats and Jonathan were inseparable again, and Scrappy remembered he was a herd dog. Since the only predator had sailed, there were no worries.

Coronel now was relieved that the Captain was gone, and he hoped that soon help might come. Perhaps the Captain would send someone? Either way, everyone was much more relaxed.

While Coronel and Jonathan were running around the island together gathering samples they hungered for fish. Gathering plant samples is hard work, especially in the heat. While they rested under a shady little palm, Coronel remembered how his family fished the river with spears made from palms.

He carefully stripped a palm leaf down to reveal a very sharp point. Then he tore apart the leaves to make abrasive reeds, which he wove together into a better mat than the one they made earlier.

They went down to the tide pools and blocked off the exit while spear fishing in the pool. It worked much better than before, and they caught a good sized fish. There was even some for Scrappy. The goats didn't care for fish at all, but the chickens did and were happy about it.

The goats got to walk on the beach and munched on seaweed. Jonathan and Coronel tried seaweed too, and found it delicious. Most seaweed is edible. Scrappy did not like it. The chickens found a crab, and spent the rest of the afternoon attempting to catch another.

Crabs are used to watching out for birds, and seagulls are much faster than chickens. Now that there are only two humans to feed on the island and they are better at fishing, the changing seasons were almost forgotten about. Both guys were as happy as they have been the whole time since the disaster.

A ship

One windy morning Jonathan woke to the sound of high surf. The waves beat against the cliffs on the backside of the island and blew wet spray all the way to the hut. It was cold, and Jonathan did not have much clothing.

He snuggled with Scrappy to help stop the shivering. When he finally felt warm enough, he walked to the beach where he saw tall clouds on the horizon. The memory of the changing seasons returned with an urgency.

He walked to Coronel's camp and they discussed their fears of the changing weather, though neither had a plan. They had not been there long enough to know what to expect. They discussed how they might use the crates to build a better shelter and maybe use sand to anchor the sides and shelter it from the wind. Too bad all the large timbers were gone.

The wind blew and while they talked they would occasionally have to jump up to chase something it had blown away. Scrappy thought it a fun game, but Coronel and Jonathan would have been happy to let him play alone. When Scrappy did fetch something, it took flight as soon as he released it. And, of course, he immediately resumed the chase.

Fishing in the wind was almost impossible, so the guys settled for fruit and later a glass of milk before bed. The goats had become used to their pen and insisted on being secured in it at night. It probably made them feel safer or perhaps it reminded them of their barn back home. The wind continued to blow as darkness fell and sleep came easily to the sound of leaves rustling and waves crashing.

Half drowsy, Jonathan was startled by the out-of-breath calls from Coronel. "What, what is happening here?" Jonathan asks, as Scrappy lets out three very loud barks. "I, I think, it's a ship, I'm almost certain, we have to signal it before it leaves." Coronel bends over, panting from the exhausting run. Scrappy must have understood because he was already half way to the beach, still barking in sets of three. WOOF! WOOF! WOOF!

Jonathan scrambled and quickly dressed while running to the beach. Coronel could not keep up. Down on the beach it was confirmed, it was, indeed, a ship. It was too far away to see any flags. It was not wise to summon unknown ships, even when stranded, but the excitement was too much to bear.

Jonathan was already making a large fire pile when Coronel finally arrived on the beach. They struggled to get the fire going in the wind and ocean spray, while Scrappy barked as loud as he could at the distant ship.

It seemed like it took a very long time to light that fire and it was amazing that they could still see the ship when they finally got some flames and smoke. Once the fire was going well they added seaweed to make thick smoke so that they would be more visible. They fanned the flames and smoke with the mat they made to trap fish and waved their arms as if trying to fly.

All that work, barking and jumping up and down did not seem to get any attention from the ship. Did they not see that smoke? How could you miss it? They were yelling as loud as they could and frantically fanning the smoke. They did not know whether to laugh or cry. "Oh, please let them see us," they both kept saying. Scrappy ran back and forth barking, still in sets of three. That means it's serious!

After about an hour, the ship seemed to slowly move. At first it looked as though the ship was getting further away, but then it looked like it was getting closer. The two survivors were so tired they had almost given up. They were still not sure if the ship saw them, so they had to keep making smoke and waving. Scrappy was losing his voice.

He had not barked much lately and he was getting tired, too.

As they watched in hope the ship began to get larger and larger sailing toward them. Relief came as they knew it was definitely responding to them. As the ship came closer, they became uneasy. Who are they? They worried.

Did the Captain send the ship? Are they English, Spanish, Portuguese, or French? Where are they going, where will they take us, are they going to take us? All these questions would soon be answered, but it may be too late to refuse a visit.

As the ship approached it turned with the wind and sailed straight at the island. No flags were visible. It seemed a solid ship and sat well in the waves and had large sails, but was only using one and partially at that, then none. Soon the ship dropped anchor and pivoted on the line to face the bow into the wind. The ship was now close enough to see men moving on deck. They were coming.

A boat was lowered into the water and several men rowed toward the island. They were not far from the ship when a Skull and Crossbones flag was raised on the main mast. Pirates! PIRATES!

Pirates!

"Oh No! Now what do we do? RUN! But wait, this is a small island, they are going to find us!" There was no point in running. Besides, what if they leave? The guys would still be ship-wrecked. "Let's just hope they are going to help us," Jonathan suggested. Coronel worried about the pirates, but they were coming. Scrappy barked at the boat as it came over the waves, one breaker at a time.

Jonathan and Coronel waved and nervously faced the pirates. The closer the pirates got, the more the tension built. Jonathan gathered things to offer them. When they finally pulled the small boat ashore, the pirates looked sickly. Jonathan ran toward their boat and helped pull it ashore.

The pirates had badly chapped lips and looked ill. "Water?" one asked in a raspy, sad voice. "Yes! "Jonathan replied, and gave them water. The first pirate drank half the water and passed it to another. Jonathan knew they needed more and he went to get more. The pirates were happy to drink and expressed gratitude to Coronel and Jonathan. "You mates have saved our lives," they told Jonathan as he handed them another flask of water.

The pirates filled a small barrel of water and took it back to the ship. Some pirates stayed on the island while the boat shuttled more of the crew to the island. Jonathan prepared food. Coronel is trying very hard to catch a lot of fish. The survivors, Coronel and Jonathan, agree not to tell the pirates about the goats and chickens just yet.

More and more sick pirates came ashore and were given water. Soon they are fed fish cooked over the fire and fruit and berries served on palm quills. Within a few hours the pirates looked much better. "Scurvy dawgs the lot of us, 'til ye saved us mates." one of the pirates proclaimed, followed by a loud pirate cheer to honor Jonathan and Coronel.

While Jonathan brought water and fruit for the pirates to replenish their strength, Coronel and some of the pirates went to the tide pools to fish. They needed so much food that almost every fish was a "keeper". Before the sun went down, all the pirates had full bellies and smiling faces. They had gone a long time without fruit and it was making them sick. Not having fresh water almost killed them.

As they all ate together, the long pirate faces turned to smiles. They were not all that scary after all. It didn't take long and some pirates started singing. Jonathan had no idea what they were singing, but most of them seemed to know the words.

Scrappy joined in with an occasional howl, which drew deep laughter from several pirates. "He's one of us," they said and gave him some fish. Scrappy loved the attention, especially being fed. The pirates all bedded down on the beach after eating, but by dark they had all returned to their ship.

Pirates don't sleep well on land. They promised to return in the morning, and said they would not leave without filling their barrels with water and storing fruit for their journey. For now, a long day was coming to an end, and Jonathan forgot to feed the chickens and goats in all the excitement. They were still put up from the previous night.

When he got back to his hut, they were anxiously awaiting him. He fed them all from scraps he managed to bring back from the day's meals. The day brought many changes, but as yet, few answers.

The stars twinkled brightly that night despite a near full moon setting just after twilight. Jonathan went to sleep looking up at the Milky Way and thinking about whether he would go with the pirates or stay on the island, and he wondered if Coronel would go or stay as well.

In the morning the pirates came back as promised. They brought many barrels that smelled more of wine and ale than water and they filled them by the waterfall without rinsing them. It took a long time to row back to the ship with a full boat. You cannot fill a boat with water and expect it to float. Therefore, it took several trips.

While the pirates were ferrying the water, Jonathan tried to find out where they were going, and where they were from. He wanted to see if they could help him get off the island, or if he was better off staying. Coronel seemed anxious about the future as well, and he was not sure if he would even be allowed on the ship, much less have it take him where he wanted to go.

Jonathan was not sure where he wanted to go. The island was his home for now. He felt safe, but did not know what the weather would bring. Maybe he could trade the pirates for some clothes. Was it possible to go with the pirates and not become a pirate?

"Where are you going?' Jonathan asked one of the pirates."

"All the same place, if the Nuns are right," the pirate answered, and all the other pirates laughed.

"But where are you sailing the ship to?" Jonathan countered. But nobody answered.

"Back to the boat," one of them finally said. They each picked up a barrel and waddled toward the little boat with it, shuffling warm sand through their toes as they walked down the beach, Scrappy and Jonathan following.

"Where are you going?" a pirate asked as they walk.

"The New World!" Jonathan answered, not knowing if he should have said that since he did not know where he was going. He just trusted that his family was going there. He did not know what that will look like. He tried to explain it to the pirate, but each answer turned into another question. He had to admit that he did not know where he was going, or how to get there.

The pirate said that they were in the tropics and that was good place to stay, with warm seas and a mild winter. That was good news for Jonathan who was worried about winter coming.

Coronel saw the pirates as an answer to his prayer. He wanted to have the pirates take his crates to the place where he was taken from as a child. He wanted to get off the island now.

While Jonathan was helping with the water and talking to those men, Coronel was smooth talking another group into letting him go with them to a place at least on the South American continent. They did not acknowledge knowing of a port called Coronel, which was the last sign Coronel saw, before sailing off to Europe as a small boy. He assumed it as his name, so that he would never forget it.

They joked and poked fun at Coronel, but didn't promise or deny the possibility of passage. It seemed that nobody was really in charge. Coronel became more frustrated but it would do no good to get upset. How do you negotiate with a bunch of guys that just joke around and laugh at you?

Do these guys have a leader? Is there a Captain to this ship? Where are these guys going? Will I have to join their group to get on the ship? Is there enough room for all my cargo? All these questions were racing through Coronel's head as the pirates merrily mused at Coronel's curiosity. They gave no answers, and answered every question with a question.

Their small boat made several trips with water and food for their impending departure and Coronel noted its sea worthiness. It would easily be able to ferry the crates to the ship, especially in the morning calm. It was certainly possible to get everything off the island, if an agreement could be reached. Coronel did not know anything he could offer to the pirates to make them want to do anything for him. After all, if pirates want something, they usually just take it.

Distrust is not going to get him off the island. He had to find a way to convince the pirates to let him go. He also wondered what Jonathan wants to do. The decision to get on a ship with pirates was not one he wanted to make for Jonathan. It is dangerous to be on a pirate ship even if you are a pirate, but it is no place for a young lad. At that time Coronel had no idea what Jonathan wanted to do, but assumed that he would go too.

"Where am I going?" There were so many questions to ask before getting on a pirate ship. Jonathan made the island livable. If Coronel and the pirates leave, he still has Scrappy, the goats and chickens and he does not have to share them with anyone else. They would definitely be safe for now. There is always the changing weather to worry about later, but at least the pirates said it would be a mild winter. The Captain left enough material to shore up his shelter and the plants show decades of lush growth making

70

a deadly winter unlikely.

Jonathan really would like to get off the island, but he is not at all sure about getting on a pirate ship. The pirates could be hung if they're caught. Their ship could be sunk in a battle. There was no certainty in the life of a pirate, and no condemnation in staying on the island.

In contemplation, he realized that he had built everything he needed in a totally new world that nobody else had ever been to. He had done in his own way what his family set out to do, despite disaster and disadvantage. And he had saved the lives of those pirates and fed two others for months. He and his animals were survivors, not pirates and his dreams and successes are right in front of him wherever he may be.

And he will…

Survive.

www.ingramcontent.com/pod-product-compliance
Lightning Source LLC
Chambersburg PA
CBHW071201130626
46555CB00004B/1537